TWISTED TALES

Richard
Tulloch

illustrated by
Terry Denton

To whatever your name is.
Welcome to the world of stories – R.T.

For Spud! – T.D.

A Random House book

Published by Random House Australia Pty Ltd
Level 3, 100 Pacific Highway, North Sydney NSW 2060
www.randomhouse.com.au

First published by Random House in 2008

Addresses for companies within the Random House Group can be found at
www.randomhouse.com.au/offices.

National Library of Australia
Cataloguing-in-Publication Entry

Tulloch, Richard
Twisted tales/author, Richard Tulloch; illustrator, Terry Denton.
ISBN: 978 1 74166 274 0 (pbk.)
For primary age children
Denton, Terry, 1950–
A823.4

Cover illustration by Terry Denton
Cover, internal design & typesetting by Anna Warren, Warren Ventures
Printed and bound by Griffin Press, South Australia

Random House Australia uses papers that are natural, renewable and
recyclable products and made from wood grown in sustainable forests. The
logging and manufacturing processes are expected to conform to the
environmental regulations of the country of origin.

10 9 8 7 6 5 4 3 2 1

CONTENTS

It's just not fair!

Why are wolves in fairytales always bad, and witches always ugly? Because people who write fairytales don't like wolves and witches. If wolves and witches wrote books, they'd make themselves the good, beautiful heroes, and the villains would be horrible little children and wicked princes and ugly princesses.

You see, a story can be twisted by the person who tells it. Nobody likes to admit they've done something stupid, mean or downright criminal. So when they tell the story later, they leave out the embarrassing bits to try to make themselves look good and to show that, if something went wrong, it was somebody else's fault.

I've heard these stories lots of times, and so have you. I often thought the versions I heard didn't make much sense. I wasn't there when any of these stories took place. I don't know for sure who was right and who was wrong. So I just looked at the facts and asked myself whether there might have been a better explanation for what happened.

I hope you'll agree with me.

THE LIZARD'S TALE

Maybe you think it would be cool to put on a party dress, ride in a carriage and go to a ball in a palace, especially if a really cute prince was going to be there. But not everyone likes dressing up and carriages and balls and palaces . . .

Long, long ago, a lizard called Lennie
lived in a garden behind a big house. It
was a nice garden, with warm rocks for
basking on, agapanthus bushes for
sleeping under, and lots of delicious
snails. Lennie loved eating snails – crisp
and crunchy on the outside, smooth and
slimy on the inside. Yum!

Late one afternoon, Lennie was settling
down for a snooze under an agapanthus
bush, when . . . bang! went the back
door. Into the garden came a horrible
dirty giant. She was really disgusting. She
wore a revolting old sack for a dress, and
her hair was tangled and greasy and her
face was smeared with grime as if she
hadn't washed it for a month.

Lennie pressed himself deep into the
agapanthus, but the sackdress giant was

too quick for him. Her dirty bare feet
kicked the leaves aside. She grabbed
Lennie by the tail and carried him inside.
Bang! went the back door again.
It was dark in the kitchen of the big
house, but when his eyes grew used to the

light, Lennie saw there was a whole crowd
in there. There was another lizard and six
mice and a rat called Ferdi, whom Lennie
knew slightly because he lived in the
garden compost bin.

There was another giant too, a wrinkly old giant, carrying an enormous pink club with a sharp silver star on the end. The wrinkly giant whacked Lennie over the head with her club. There was an enormous puff of pɪɴᴋ sᴍᴏᴋᴇ and, next thing Lennie knew, he was growing. His legs became longer, and his tail became shorter. His smooth comfortable skin was stretched so tight it seemed to choke him. Suddenly he was covered with tight leggings and a velvet jacket, and a stiff collar prickled around his neck. His head shot up towards the ceiling, then stopped, leaving him eyeball to eyeball with the wrinkly giant.

'What is going on????'
exclaimed Lennie.

The wrinkly giant said, 'Don't worry, dear. I just changed you into a footman.'

'Well, you can change me back right now,' said Lennie. 'I didn't ask to be a footman. I don't even know what a footman is.'

'I'll change you back when the clock strikes twelve,' said the wrinkly giant. 'Till then, you have a job to do. Hang on the back of the coach and when it stops at the palace, open the door for the lady.'

'What's a palace?' asked Lennie.

'What's a job?' asked the other lizard.

But by then the wrinkly giant was busy whacking a pumpkin with the pink club. She whacked the mice, and she whacked Ferdi the Rat too. The pumpkin became a coach with Ferdi as the driver, and the poor little mice turned into 𝒽𝓊𝓰ℯ 𝒽𝒾𝒹ℯℴ𝓊𝓈 𝓌𝒽𝒾𝓉ℯ 𝒽ℴ𝓇𝓈ℯ𝓈, harnessed in a line in front of it.

Then the wrinkly giant whacked the sackdress giant with the pink club and guess what happened to her? All her clothes fell off! One more whack of the pink stick and she had new clothes, and her hair was shiny and she was wearing glass slippers with silver toecaps.

'All aboard,' said the wrinkly giant. She winked and smiled, as if this was all great fun.

Then she raised her pink club again. Lennie and the other lizard footman quickly climbed on the back of the coach and hung on, just as the wrinkly giant had told them. Ferdi the Rat cracked a whip and the mice started running for their lives. They didn't want to get whacked again.

The ride was terrifying. Lennie had never moved so fast in his whole life.

They clattered through the town on the bouncy cobblestones and Lennie hung on. They wheeled around a corner and he was still hanging on.

They bounced across a bridge and Lennie was hanging on as hard as he could.

Then they swung off the road through a set of huge iron gates and stopped in front of the biggest building Lennie had ever seen, with turrets and towers, and windows glittering with the light of a million candles.

'If you ask me, this is the palace,'
muttered Lennie. He got down off the
coach, and opened the door for the
sackdress giant. Without so much as a
please or thank you, she ran click
clickety click on her glass slippers,
up the stairs and into the palace, and the
door shut behind her.

After that things became really boring. The lizard footmen and the horse mice and Ferdi the Rat waited by the coach. Through the palace windows they could see the giants, eating and drinking and spinning round as if they'd gone mad. At one point the sackdress giant came out onto the balcony with a boy giant. They stuck their sloppy mouths together and dribbled on each other's tongues. It was the most revolting thing Lennie had ever seen.

Then they went back in again, and Lennie had nothing to do and nobody was offering him anything to eat. 'I've had enough of this,' said Lennie. He set off for a walk round the palace garden.

The garden was huge. There were shaded paths winding between sparkling fountains with lamps under the water. There were deep, dark beds of ferns and clumps of cliveas and bromeliads. 'Perfect hiding places for juicy snails,' thought Lennie. He licked his lips. And he discovered something about his tongue. It was long. Really, really long.

Lennie flicked out his tongue and used it to explore around the roots of a clivea clump. In no time, a big juicy snail crawled onto the tip of his tongue. Lennie rolled it back into his mouth. Crisp and crunchy on the outside, smooth and slimy on the inside. Yum!

For the next few hours, Lennie enjoyed a feast like he'd never had before. He slurped up slugs and crunched up caterpillars, and even picked flying moths out of the air as they fluttered in the light from the fountains.

Then suddenly he heard Bong! Bong! Bong! The clock was striking twelve. Lennie looked up from the bottom of the garden in time to see the palace doors fly open. The sackdress giant raced down the palace steps and tumbled into the coach. Ferdi the Rat cracked his whip.

'Hey, wait for me!' called Lennie. He tried to run, but he was so fat and slow from eating that by the time he got to the palace steps the coach was crunching out through the heavy iron gates.

Bonggg! The clock stopped chiming. Lennie's clothes fell off. And he shrank back into his comfortable little lizard skin in no time at all.

Just then a crowd of giants charged out the palace yelling, 'Who is she? Where did she go?'

They swarmed all around Lennie with their huge heavy feet. He knew he had to hide or he'd be stomped flatter than a slug under a lawn roller. His sharp eye caught sight of something on the steps. It was one of the sackdress giant's glass slippers. Lennie dived into it, and curled himself right down in the silver toecap.

A huge ugly hand picked up the slipper and a giant's voice boomed out,

'Whomever this slipper fits, shall be my bride!'

The next few days were the worst that Lennie could remember. They were really horrible.

Every girl giant in town wanted to stick her foot into the glass slipper on top of Lennie. Knobbly feet, stinking dirty feet, feet with smelly nail polish that nearly made him pass out. Feet with bloody blisters and bunions and cheesy stuff between the toes. Feet with green muck under the toenails. Lennie was pushed and prodded and poked and pricked. Of course, none of the feet could fit into the slipper, because Lennie was curled up in the end.

At last they came to a house where two girl giants lived, and they were the ugliest giants of all. One was so desperate to make her foot fit into the slipper that she took a kitchen knife and cut her toes off. Even then her foot was too big. The other ugly giant tried next. She squeezed and squeezed and Lennie could tell she wasn't going to give up before she crushed him to death. So he bit her toe. 'Yiiiiii!' screamed the giant, and she kicked off the glass slipper. It flew out the door and clattered down the steps into the garden, coming to rest under an agapanthus bush.

16

Lennie looked through the smudgy glass and saw . . . his own garden! There were the mice, and Ferdi the Rat too.

Before he could say anything, a huge bare foot kicked the agapanthus leaves aside. Towering above Lennie was the disgusting sackdress giant who had got him into all the trouble in the first place. She still had the **filthiest feet in the whole world**. Lennie didn't want to be stuck in a slipper with a foot like that, no way. So he hopped out of the slipper and watched as the sackdress giant slid her foot into it.

Well, of course it was easy now that
Lennie wasn't in there. Anybody could
have done it. But all the other giants knelt
down in front of the sackdress giant as if
she'd just done something brilliant.

But Lennie paid no attention to the
bowing and the trumpets and the cries of
'All hail, Queen Cinderella.'

He was just pleased to be home.

WHAT HAPPENED EVER AFTER . . .

Cinderella married the handsome prince, but remember he'd only chosen her because of her shoe size, so maybe he didn't really love her. In any case, she hated being a princess and it didn't work out.

After they got divorced, Cinderella wrote a bestselling book about cooking, cleaning and removing stains from furniture, which was what she was really good at. She married a handsome cookbook editor and lived happily ever after.

The prince married one of Cinderella's stepsisters and they both lived very miserably ever after.

THE BIG GOOD WOLF

In a land far, far away, there once lived a Big Good Wolf called Wilbur. Wilbur was generous and gentle and kind to children and he often helped old ladies across the street. Unfortunately, selfish people sometimes took advantage of Wilbur's good heart, as we'll see in this next sad tale . . .

Wilbur was really, really hungry.
He was too kind to hunt furry little
animals, so he hadn't eaten for days.

Then Wilbur smelled the most delicious
smell wafting on the breeze. Wilbur
followed the smell and found it was

coming from a basket, perched on a log,
in a clearing in a forest. Sitting beside the
basket was a little girl in a cape with a red
hood. She was crying.

Wilbur stepped up behind her. 'Why are you crying, little girl?' he asked.

The little girl didn't look up, but just sobbed, 'I was going to my grandma's cottage on the other side of the forest. I strayed off the path to pick her some pretty flowers, and now I'm lost.'

Wilbur put a gentle paw around her shoulders. 'Never mind, little girl, I'll help you.'

The little girl looked up into Wilbur's warm, kindly eyes. 'Eeeeeeeek! You're a **wolf**!' she screamed.

'It's all right,' said Wilbur, 'I'm a big good wolf. I'm generous and gentle, and kind to children and old people.'

'That's what wolves always say!' said the little girl, grabbing a stick and poking it in Wilbur's direction. 'You pretend to be friendly and then, when people aren't looking, you eat them up.'

'If I really wanted to eat you up,' said Wilbur, 'I wouldn't bother being friendly. Do you want me to show you where the path is?'

'All right, Wolf,' sniffed the little girl suspiciously.

Wilbur picked up her basket and led her to where they could see a path winding through the trees. The little girl snatched the basket back from Wilbur's paws and ran out onto the path without even thanking him.

'Um, that's *a* path,' called Wilbur, 'but it leads the long way round. I could show you my 𝔰𝔭𝔢𝔠𝔦𝔞𝔩 𝔰𝔥𝔬𝔯𝔱 𝔠𝔲𝔱 through the forest if you like.'

'Course I don't like!' said the girl. 'I know the way from here, and if I hadn't wasted time talking to you, I'd be halfway there by now.' She started off down the path. The smell from her basket dangled in the air and Wilbur remembered how hungry he was. He walked alongside the little girl for a few steps.

'There's no need to follow me, Wolf,' she said rudely.

'I was just wondering what was in the basket,' said Wilbur.

'An apple pie for Grandma, if you must know,' said the girl.

'I can smell sausage,' said Wilbur.

'The sausage is for my lunch,' she said.

'I'm sorry to bother you,' said Wilbur, 'but I'm really very hungry and I wonder if you could spare just a little piece . . .'

'Stop pestering me, Wolf!' snapped the girl as she strode off down the path.

Wilbur wandered back into the forest, hoping to find a few fallen nuts or a mushroom that he could eat. But he couldn't find anything at all . . .

. . . until he came upon a man sitting on a log, laughing to himself and singing:

> *'I'm a jolly woodcutter,*
> *as jolly as can be,*
> *I think of jolly funny jokes*
> *when I cut down a tree!'*

The man seemed to think this was hilarious. He took a thick sandwich from his lunch box and stuffed it into his mouth. Then he started laughing again and sprayed ham and tomato all down his front.

He stopped laughing when he saw Wilbur.

'Excuse me, jolly woodcutter,' said Wilbur, 'but I'm a very hungry big good wolf. I wonder if you could spare one of your sandwiches.'

The jolly woodcutter
snapped his lunch box shut. 'I'll tell
you a very funny joke,' he said. 'It
starts like this. I have three
sandwiches left. You can have them
if you cut down that tree for me.'
He pointed to a large dead oak tree
that stood nearby.

'That's not a funny
joke,' said Wilbur.

'It will be,' said the jolly
woodcutter. 'Cut down the tree and
I'll tell you the funny part later.'

Wilbur picked up the jolly
woodcutter's heavy axe. It was hard
to cut dead solid wood and it took
him a long time to chop, but
at last down came the tree
with a mighty crash.

When Wilbur turned round, the jolly woodcutter had eaten one of the sandwiches and was laughing fit to burst, spraying cheese and lettuce over his knees.

'Hey!' said Wilbur.

'Don't fyew flurry, Folf,' said the woodcutter, with his mouth full of cheese and lettuce. 'There are still two more sandwiches. They're yours if you saw up that wood for me.'

Wilbur was naturally rather annoyed with the way the woodcutter had broken his promise. But he didn't like arguments. So he picked up the woodcutter's heavy saw, and dragged it back and forth across the fallen tree. It was 𝔥𝖺𝗋𝖽 𝗐𝗈𝗋𝗄 and it took him a long time, but at last he had

a pile of logs cut and loaded into the jolly woodcutter's wheelbarrow.

But when Wilbur turned round again, the jolly woodcutter had eaten a second sandwich and was laughing so much that a gob of peanut butter flew out and landed on his foot.

'That's not fair,' said Wilbur.

'It's jolly funny, though,' said the jolly woodcutter.

Wilbur didn't think it was very funny at all. 'You said you'd give me three sandwiches if I cut the tree, and you've eaten two yourself. You give me the last sandwich right now.'

'You want to hear the really funny bit at the end of the joke?' said the jolly woodcutter.

'No,' said Wilbur, 'just give me the sandwich, please.'

The jolly woodcutter tipped his lunch box upside down. It was empty.

'The really funny bit is, I only had *two* sandwiches left,' laughed the jolly woodcutter, 'and I've eaten them both. So you've cut all that wood for nothing! What a great joke!'

He slapped his knee and laughed till the tears rolled down his cheeks.

Wilbur the big good wolf didn't laugh with him. He thought about those sandwiches and how good they would have been in his empty belly. A slobber of drool crawled out of the corner of his mouth and dripped towards the ground,

even though he tried to lick it back in with his tongue.

The jolly woodcutter saw this and suddenly became a little nervous.

'Er, don't worry, Wolf,' he said. 'I was cutting this wood for an old lady who lives on the other side of the forest. She pays me with the most delicious scones you ever tasted. If you deliver the wood for me, you can have the scones.'

'Promise?' asked Wilbur.

'Scout's honour,' said the jolly woodcutter, crossing his heart and hoping he wouldn't die.

Wilbur pushed the heavy wheelbarrow through the forest, using his special short cut. At last he came to a cheerful little cottage from which came the most delicious smell of freshly baked scones.

'Wood delivery!' called Wilbur.

'Oh lovely, my dear,' called an old lady's voice. 'Bring it through to my bedroom.'

Wilbur opened the door. A very fat old lady was sitting up in bed with a frilly bonnet on her head.

'I'd get up and help you,' said the old lady, 'but I'm a poor old grandma tired out from baking all morning.'

Wilbur staggered into the room with an armful of wood.

'Hello, Woodcutter,' said the old lady, reaching down beside the bed to find her glasses, because she was rather short-sighted. 'What a big nose you've got!'

'All the better to smell with,' said Wilbur, kicking the glasses under the cupboard. He was worried the old lady might get a fright if she saw a wolf in her bedroom. 'Do I smell . . . scones?' he asked, in his most friendly voice.

'You certainly do, my dear,' said the old lady. 'Exactly one hundred, and I've eaten them all.'

Wilbur dropped his wood on the floor. 'Did you say you ate *all* the scones?' he gasped.

'Well, I've only eaten ninety-nine so far,' said the old lady, popping the last scone into her mouth. 'But that's the hundredth. Once I start eating them I can't sto . . . op-uchhh!'

Suddenly the old lady choked on the last scone. Wilbur rushed to slap her on the back and tried to clear her throat, but it was too late. The old lady died in his arms. She looked horrible – very fat, blue in the face and with scone crumbs all down her front.

Just then there was a knock on the door, and a voice from outside called, 'Yoo-hoo! Grandma!'

Wilbur peeped through a crack in the curtain. It was the little girl with her basket of goodies.

'That poor little girl!' thought the big good wolf. 'She was mean to me in the forest but that was probably because she knew children shouldn't talk to strangers. I'll have to make sure she doesn't get a terrible shock from seeing her grandma dead, with a horrible blue face and scone crumbs all over her! There's only one thing to do . . . '

Wilbur quickly ate the old lady. She tasted 𝔥𝔬𝔯𝔯𝔦𝔟𝔩𝔢, even though Wilbur was so very hungry. Then he slipped on the old lady's bonnet, jumped into bed and pulled the covers around his chin. He thought, 'I'll pretend to be Grandma till

the little girl goes away. Then I'll leave her a note pretending it's from Grandma. I'll say I love her very much but I'm going for a holiday in a beautiful sunny place and staying there forever.'

He dimmed the light so that it wasn't quite so obvious that he wasn't an old lady, and called, 'Come in, my dear.'

The little girl came in and peered at Wilbur through the gloom. 'Ooh, Grandma, what big eyes you have!'

'Um, all the better to see you with, my dear,' said Wilbur, in his best imitation of the old lady's voice, 'but it's not very polite to make such personal remarks.'

The girl would not be stopped. She went on: 'And what big ears you have and your face is all hairy and you've got bad breath and what terrible ugly big sticky-out teeth you have!'

'Er, all the better to eat you with,' said Wilbur. He didn't mean to say anything nasty and cruel, but it just accidentally slipped out.

The little girl came close and peered into Wilbur's kind, smiling face. 'Eeeeeek! You're a wolf!' she screamed. 'You've eaten Grandma!'

'Y-yes, I d-did,' stammered Wilbur, but before he could explain, the girl ran and hid in the wardrobe.

Just then there was another knock at the door.

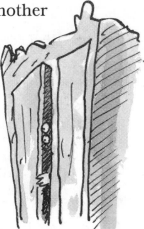

'Knock knock!'

'Who's there?' called Wilbur.

'Boo!' said a voice.

'Boo who?' asked Wilbur.

'What are you crying for, you little baby?' said the jolly woodcutter.

He thought this was hilarious. He slapped his sides and doubled over and laughed and laughed.

The little girl burst out of the cupboard and ran to open the door. 'Help! I'm being attacked by a horrible big wolf! Kill him! Cut out his liver! Shish-kebab his kidneys! Chop his head off with your axe!'

Wilbur ran out the door and hid deep in the forest.

'It's not fair!' thought Wilbur. 'I've tried so hard to be kind and to help people. But everyone's been nasty to me, and now I've got a bellyache from eating a fat mean old lady and running too soon after lunch. I don't think I want to be a big good wolf any more.'

Just then he came upon another little cottage. It was a very strange little cottage, and from it came the most delicious smell. Wilbur looked in through the window and saw something he knew would be lovely to eat.

The cottage door was shut tight, but the house was built of straw.

'Little Pig, Little Pig, let me come in,' called Wilbur, the Big Bad Wolf . . .

WHAT HAPPENED EVER AFTER . . .

Wilbur wasn't a big bad wolf for very long. He enjoyed eating little pigs, but after he'd tried his first two, a little pig in a brick house played a nasty trick on him, which landed him in hot water. You may have read something about it. The sneaky little pig said Wilbur was dead, but really he ran away and joined a brass band, where he now huffs and puffs into a tuba, and nobody cares how big his ears are.

When Little Red Riding Hood grew up, naturally she married the jolly woodcutter. He drove her crazy with his silly jokes, and it served her right.

SWEET DREAMS, BRIAR-ROSE!

Where is your favourite place in the world? Maybe on a lovely beach, or the top of a high mountain with a beautiful view, or on the sports field when your team is winning? But if you're being really honest, wouldn't you sometimes rather be fast asleep in a nice warm bed?

In a far-off kingdom, in a fairytale castle all covered with vines, there once lived a princess as beautiful as the day is long. Her name was Briar-Rose. Briar-Rose had long dark hair and long dark eyelashes fluttering over beautiful dark eyes. But under her beautiful dark eyes were long dark shadows, for Briar-Rose could not sleep.

It may be fun to stay up late, and even to party all night once in a while. But if

you had to stay awake all the time, as Briar-Rose did, you wouldn't like it one little bit.

Briar-Rose did try to get to sleep. Every night she climbed up the winding staircase to her bedroom in the highest tower of the palace. But while the king and queen and all the servants drifted straight off to **Dreamland**, the princess just tossed and turned. She flipped her pillow over and over, till it was twisted into a knot. She stared at the ceiling for hours, and sometimes leaned out her window to gaze on the sleeping town under the night sky, wishing that she could doze off like all the other people in the kingdom.

When morning came, Briar-Rose would look at herself in the mirror and see the dark shadows under her eyes. She'd climb down the winding staircase and be **tired** and **irritable** for the whole day.

The king and queen tried every trick they could think of to get their daughter to sleep.

'I know,' said the queen. 'I'll invite the finest musicians in the land to play gentle, soothing lullabies outside her bedroom door. Maybe that will help.'

She sent for the kingdom's best flautist, harpist and violinist. As soon as the princess retired for the night they began to play. The music that drifted down from the tower was so gentle and soothing that the king and queen fell asleep at once, and the servants fell asleep soon after them. But the next to fall asleep was the harpist, and the violinist and flautist weren't far behind. Princess Briar-Rose was still wide awake.

'How about this,' said the king next morning. 'I'll get the worst court jester in the land to tell her some jokes.'

'Telling jokes will never send the princess to sleep!' said the queen.

'Billy Silly's jokes are really bad,' said the king. 'They're so boring they send me to sleep in five minutes.'

So the next night, Billy Silly climbed up the winding staircase to tell jokes to the princess. 'What time does a dragon come out to fight?' he asked.

'I don't know,' sighed the princess.

'Knight time!' chuckled Billy Silly. 'How many jesters does it take to change a candle?' The princess was already too bored to say she didn't know. 'Jester one!' said Billy Silly. He laughed his head off at this terrible joke, but the princess yawned.

Billy Silly's jokes went on and on. He told 'knock, knock' jokes and 'Why did the ogre cross the road' jokes ('To get to the ogre side!' was the answer). When morning came, Billy Silly had bored himself to sleep, because even he couldn't be bothered listening to such bad jokes. Princess Briar-Rose was still wide awake.

Every night, the king and queen tried a new scheme to get the princess to sleep. They asked the royal cook to make her endless cups of hot chocolate. They had the royal pillow-stuffer make her the softest goose-down pillows. They were so desperate they even asked the royal shepherd to bring a flock of sheep up the winding staircase so that Briar-Rose could count them. That was a really silly idea, but it shows how desperate the king and queen had become. The sheep made a dreadful noise in the bedroom, and one of them even tried to eat a goose-down pillow. Princess Briar-Rose was awake all night and the next night too, cleaning up the mess they left behind.

Then one day, a little old woman, shrivelled and brown as a walnut, knocked on the palace door. 'I can send the princess to sleep,' she said.

Naturally the king and queen invited her in at once. 'How can you send her to sleep?' asked the king. 'Do you sing lullabies or make chocolate milk drinks?'

'No,' said the shrivelled old woman, 'I'll teach her to spin flax.' She unpacked a spinning wheel.

'Of course!' said the queen. 'I'd forgotten all about that. Why didn't we think of it before?'

'How will spinning flax help the princess to sleep?' asked the king.

'Shh!' said the queen. 'Just watch.'

No sooner had Briar-Rose sat down at the spinning wheel, than she pricked her finger on the sharp end of the spindle. 'Ou . . . !' exclaimed the princess. She was going to say 'ouch' but, before she got to the end of the word, she fell to the floor and lay there, fast asleep.

The king jumped up and grabbed the shrivelled old woman by her shrivelled old shoulders. 'You've killed her! That was a poisoned spindle!'

'No,' said the queen, 'Briar-Rose isn't dead. She's just asleep. Don't you remember? When she was a baby, a witch told her that if she ever pricked her finger with a spindle she would fall asleep. I'd forgotten all about it myself but now the prophecy has come true! It seemed silly at the time because you'd think that pricking your finger would wake you up. But look – it worked!'

The king thrust a bag of gold into the old woman's shrivelled hand. 'Thank you so much!' he said.

The king and queen had their servants carry the sleeping princess up the winding staircase and lay her in the bed in the tower. Briar-Rose did look very beautiful, now that she was asleep, and already the dark shadows under her eyes were starting to fade.

They closed the bedroom door and hung a sign on it: 'Do Not Disturb. Sleeping Beauty Inside.'

Then the king and queen and all the servants went to bed themselves. They were so tired from worrying about Briar-Rose that they were sure they would sleep very soundly.

Briar-Rose drifted straight to Dreamland,
where she had the most wonderful
dreams any princess had ever dreamed.
In her dreams, she ran on her bare feet
over soft moss in deep dark forests. She
splashed along the shores of long sandy
beaches where dolphins cavorted in the
waves. She soared on angel wings
and flew with the eagles over snow-capped
mountains. She rode on the back of a
zebra, galloping across a vast plain, with a
pair of friendly cheetahs loping
alongside.

The zebra brought her to a tent in the desert. In the centre of an elaborate Persian carpet, lay the most magnificent banquet Briar-Rose had ever seen. There were piles of pomegranates and mangoes and red-centred figs. There were platters of spicy meats and steaming salvers of saffron rice and bowls of pink Turkish delight.

But before the princess could taste any of this dream food, a window opened in the tent, and in flew a pig. A ḣorrible slobbering pig, with drool sliding off his snout and dripping in great puddles onto the elaborate Persian carpet.

The princess tried to back away from the disgusting flying pig, but she tripped on a pomegranate and fell back on the Persian carpet. The pig waddled over and . . . kissed her!

'Eeeeeeeeerrrrkkkk!'

The princess's scream cut the air, echoing down the winding staircase and resounding through the whole palace. In an instant the king and queen and all the servants were wide awake. They rushed up the winding staircase to the tower room.

The queen ripped the 'Do Not Disturb' sign off the door as the king fumbled for the keys. Then they burst into the room.

Briar-Rose was wide awake, holding a sheep-chewed goose-down pillow in front of her. In the far corner of the room was a young man in tights, looking very uncomfortable.

'Who are you?' demanded the king.

'I'm, um, handsome Prince Charming,' said the young man.

'That's what you say,' snorted Briar-Rose, jumping out of bed. 'And even if you were handsome, which you are not, that doesn't mean you can climb up the side of someone's castle. And what sort of person sneaks in a girl's window while she's asleep? And as for kissing me without my permission, that's just disgusting! There's absolutely nothing charming about you, and worst of all – YOU WOKE ME UP!!' She pushed the prince hard in the middle of his handsome chest.

After that, things happened very quickly. The handsome prince staggered back and fell out the window. He made two graceful double somersaults in mid-air and landed **splash!** in the moat.

The princess sighed, and pulled the spindle out from under her pillow, where the king had left it for an emergency like this. She jabbed it into her finger, and slumped back on her goose-down pillow before she could even say '**Ouch!**'.

The king and queen and all the servants sighed very big sighs, and went back down the winding staircase.

And they all slept happily ever after.

WHAT HAPPENED
EVER AFTER . . .

*The handsome prince swam to the far
side of the moat. As you may have
guessed from his two graceful double
somersaults, he wasn't really a prince.
He was a trampoline champion who'd
bounced off course through the
palace window.
He went back to working
at the circus, and never
told anyone about his adventure.
Well, he did tell a friend of a friend of my
cousin Eric, who passed the story on to
me, so that's how I know it's true.*

PARDON, PETUNIA?

Could anyone spin straw into gold? I don't think so. If anyone could spin straw into anything, it wouldn't be gold; it would more likely be those little mats people put under drinks to stop them staining the tablecloth. So there has to be a simpler explanation for that silly Rumpelstiltskin story.

A long time ago, in a land far away, a massive meteorite came hurtling out of space, fizzed through the atmosphere and landed in the middle of a town square with the most enormous

BANG!

When the dust cleared, the townsfolk edged cautiously out of their houses to look at the strange rock standing black and upright in the middle of the road. It hadn't landed on anybody or anything, and in fact had fallen in exactly the right spot to make a useful traffic roundabout. But as we'll see in a moment, it had done some damage.

Benjamin Hamhock the butcher said, 'Oh, isn't it big!'

'No, it isn't a pig,' said Solomon Rolls
the baker. 'Pigs don't fly. It's a meteorite.'

'Meet you tonight?' asked Jenny Stitch
the draper.

'It just missed my house,' said Abe
Dusty the miller.

'Come again?' said three other people.

'Abe Dusty said it just kissed his
mouse,' said Dan Shuttle the weaver.

You see what had happened, don't you?
The big **BANG!** had made everybody in
the whole town a little deaf.

For weeks afterwards, people shouted at each other until they started to lose their voices. Then they put their hands behind their ears and said, 'Eh?' or 'I beg your pardon?' or 'Would you mind repeating that?'

But as the months passed, everybody tired of shouting and asking people to repeat things. So they politely pretended to understand, even if they didn't quite catch what was said.

One fine day that led to a sad but true story . . .

👂 👂 👂 👂 👂 👂 👂

Abe Dusty the miller was delivering sacks of flour to the king's palace on the hill. With him on his cart rode his lovely daughter, Petunia. Petunia was a charming girl, pretty and hard-working, gentle and polite . . . and just as deaf as everybody else.

Now it happened that the king himself was strolling in the garden when Abe and Petunia rolled past. They recognised the king at once and bowed low. The king, who was kind and generous to his subjects, waved for them to rise.

'Your daughter is very **beautiful**,' said the king to the miller.

'Very **dutiful**, Your Majesty,' replied Abe Dusty. 'She does exactly what she's told.' Mr Dusty hadn't quite heard what the king had said about his daughter, but he politely pretended that he did. 'She's clever too. Plays chess, and she's also good at sewing.'

'Good at rowing?' said the king. 'How remarkable!' (The **bang!** had made the king deaf too.)

The miller continued, 'Oh yes, Petunia is always working with her pins and needles, making dresses we can sell for good money. Her mother always says, "Petunia's pins draw in the gold!"'

'Petunia spins straw into gold!' exclaimed the deaf king. 'That's extraordinary! Bring her to the palace this evening and she can show me.'

When Petunia arrived at the palace that night, the king gave her a sumptuous banquet, finished off with rumballs, which Petunia decided were her favourite sweets.

The king even made charming conversation, entertaining her with a very humorous story. Being a little deaf she wasn't entirely sure what the humorous story was about. It may have been about a hare called Ernie who ate carrots. Or maybe it was a bear called Bernie who ate parrots.

After dinner, the king led Petunia to a small room, with straw covering the floor. In the middle of the room was a spinning wheel. 'Now, Petunia, spin this straw into gold,' said the king.

Petunia hesitated. She couldn't believe she'd heard him right. 'Excuse me, Your Majesty, but did you say I was to . . . ?'

'Spin the straw into gold,' repeated the king in his biggest, clearest voice. 'Take all night if you want to. I'm popping off to bed.'

At this, Petunia turned white as a sheet. When the king had said 'I'm popping off to bed', she'd thought he said, 'I'm chopping off your head.' And of course she had no idea how to spin straw into gold.

As soon as the king was gone, poor Petunia burst into tears.

Just then, a $funny$ $little$ man rode past the window on a skinny donkey. 'No need to cry, young lady,' he said. 'Life isn't so bad!'

'But it is bad,' sobbed Petunia. 'The king says I have to spin this straw into gold.'

The little man put a bony finger in his ear and wiggled it around. 'Did you say you have to cling to your paws in the cold?' he asked.

'No,' sobbed Petunia loudly. 'I've been commanded to **SPIN THIS STRAW INTO GOLD**.'

'What a weird command!' said the little man.

'And if it isn't done by morning the king's **CHOPPING OFF MY HEAD**.'

The little man laid a kindly hand on her sleeve. 'That's even more weird! However, don't you worry – I'll take care of everything. But what will you give me in return?'

Petunia said, 'Take my necklace. If the king chops my head off, I won't be able to wear it anyway.'

The little man took the necklace, hung it round his own neck and sent Petunia off to bed.

Of course it's very difficult to spin straw into anything at all, and totally impossible to spin it into gold. The little man knew this but he had a plan.

First he shovelled all the straw out the window and his skinny donkey gobbled it up.

Next he crept through the palace to the royal treasury, picked the lock, and filled his pockets with gold coins. It wasn't even technically stealing, because he took the gold straight up to Petunia's room, which was still part of the king's palace. Then he climbed out the window and went on his way.

Next morning when the king opened Petunia's door, the straw was gone, and scattered around the spinning wheel were the finest gold coins, each one bearing a picture of the king himself.

Tȟe king was deligȟted. He congratulated Petunia, and rewarded her with a delicious breakfast . . . and a delicious lunch . . . and another delicious dinner, and more ꭇuᴍballs. He challenged her to a game of chess, let her win, and told her another humorous story about the time he spanked a dragon called Bruce. Or maybe it was a story about the time he drank a flagon of juice. Petunia wasn't quite sure, but she enjoyed the story anyway.

Then the king took her back to the little room. There she saw even bigger piles of straw around the spinning wheel.

'Petunia,' said the king, 'spin this straw into gold by morning and I'll put you on a pension for ten years!' Then he popped off to bed.

Petunia burst into tears. She thought the king said he'd *put her in a dungeon* for ten years.

But in through the window came the funny little man again, and once more he offered to spin the straw for her. Petunia gave him the ring from her finger, and he sent her to bed. Then he fed the straw to the donkey, robbed the treasury and left her a room full of gold.

Next morning the king was delighted,
and hugely impressed that Petunia had
not only spun the straw into gold but
she'd made an 𝑒𝑥𝑎𝑐𝑡 𝑐𝑜𝑝𝑦 of the
golden crown he'd worn at his coronation.
He was a very kind and trusting king (and
ever so slightly dim) so he didn't notice
that it *was* his real coronation crown. He
arranged for her pension to be paid,
starting the next week.

👑 👑 👑 👑 👑

That evening after dinner, chess and rumballs, the king took Petunia to her room, now filled to the ceiling with straw. 'If you can spin this into gold tonight, I'll make you my queen,' he said.

Petunia could bear this no longer. She sank to her knees in front of the king. 'Please, Your Majesty, I beg of you, don't do that. I'd be so embarrassed.'

'You'd be embarrassed if I make you my queen?' asked the king, very loudly and clearly.

Petunia blushed deeply. 'Oh, make me your *queen*', she said. 'Sorry. I thought you said you'd make me *turn green*.'

'Of course I wouldn't do that, silly,' said the king. 'Spin this straw into gold, and **I'll marry you tomorrow**.'

As soon as he was gone, Petunia burst into tears again. By now she was in love

with the king, and wanted to marry him. But of course she couldn't spin the straw into gold. Luckily, the funny little man appeared at her window.

'If you help me one more time, I could become queen,' she said. 'But I'm afraid I have nothing precious to give you. My pension won't arrive until next week.'

The little man laughed. 'That's all right. After you are queen, you will have a son.'

'So what do you want from me?' asked Petunia.

'Your prince and heir,' said the little man.

'No trouble at all!' said Petunia, surprised. She thought he said, '*You rinse my hair*,' so that was why she agreed immediately.

So the straw was fed to a very fat donkey, the treasury was robbed and the gold was scattered in the room.

The next afternoon, Petunia married the delighted king and, sure enough, as the little man had predicted, a baby boy was born. Queen Petunia and the king could not have been happier. The baby's name was Prince Ronald, but Petunia called him her little Rumball, after her favourite sweet.

👑 👑 👑 👑 👑

One day, when Prince Ronald was just a year old, Queen Petunia and her maid were playing chess. The little prince kept interrupting their game by picking pieces off the board and sitting on them, but they didn't mind because he was so cute. The queen tickled the little boy until he couldn't stop giggling. When he rolled away she'd find the missing chessman under his fat little bottom.

Suddenly there was a tapping at the window and there was the little man again.

'Come in, come in!' said the queen. She was delighted to see him again. She sent her maid out for warm water, then said to the little man, 'Take off your cap.'

'Take off my cap?' he asked. 'Whatever for?'

'A deal is a deal,' said Petunia, 'We agreed that when my baby was born, I'd give you a rinse.'

'Not a *rinse* – you agreed to give me a *prince*!' said the little man, enunciating every word very clearly so that even deaf Queen Petunia couldn't mistake what he was saying. 'You promised me your baby boy!'

Poor Petunia burst into tears again –
she'd had a lot of practice by now.
Bursting into tears must be a trick worth
learning, because again the little man took
pity on her. 'All right,' he said, patting her
kindly on the elbow. 'Don't cry. If you can
guess my name, I'll let you keep
your child.'

Queen Petunia started guessing
immediately, listing all the boys' names
she could possibly think of. 'Is your name
Bob or Jack or Kevin . . . ?'

'No, no, and no,' said the little man.

When she'd run out of names like Harry and Tom, she moved on to more unusual names. 'Are you Jeremiah or Bartholomew or Marmaduke?'

'No, no, and no,' said the little man.

All day the queen guessed at the names but the little man always said no. She started to invent names: 'Are you called Sillyshanks? Hairylegs? Bobblebottom?'

But after every name the little man just shook his head.

As the day wore on, tears rolled down Queen Petunia's cheeks. She would never guess the little man's name, and it seemed that he would take her son after all. It broke her heart to see little Prince Ronald playing there among the chess pieces, not understanding that unless a miracle happened he was going to be taken away from his dear mother.

'Is your name **Big Nose**, or **Wobble Tummy**?' she sobbed.

'No and no,' said the little man. He was hardly even listening now, and instead was shifting pieces around on the chessboard, playing a game with the prince. Then he stopped. 'Hey,' he said, 'the black king is missing!'

Queen Petunia dried her eyes with a handkerchief and reached across to tickle Prince Ronald. The child giggled and rolled off the cushion, revealing the black king lying underneath his fat bottom.

'That rotten little boy cheated!' snapped the little man. 'He hid his king just as I was going to checkmate him! Petunia put the black king back on the board. 'I'm sorry,' she sniffed. 'My baby doesn't know the rules of chess. Rumball steals kings – that's his game.'

A silence fell in the room. The little man went white as a sheet, and when he spoke, his every word rang through the room like the clear ping of a bell. 'Did you say "Rumpelstiltskin – that's his name"?'

Petunia hadn't said "Rumpelstiltskin"; she'd said "Rumball steals kings". But now she knew. 'Your name is Rumpelstiltskin!' she said.

The little man turned red, then purple with rage. He jumped up, sending the chessboard flying. 'Who told you?' he screamed. 'Nobody can guess my name!' He sprang out the window, and as he rode away on his donkey, his voice echoed through the street: 'You're a sneaky, low-down, horrible, ungrateful dirty, rotten . . .' He went on and on, calling the queen every nasty name he could think of – every one of them much too rude to go into this story.

But Queen Petunia gathered little Prince
Rumball into her arms and gave him a
massive hug, as if she would never ever
let him go. She looked out the window to
see the little man riding away into the
distance.

'Pardon?' she called.

WHAT HAPPENED
EVER AFTER . . .

Prince Ronald grew up healthy and strong and became King Ronald. He is a fine and honest king, although the courtiers say he still sometimes cheats at chess.

Rumpelstiltskin was arrested for using offensive language against the royal family. But the judge let him off with a warning after he explained that he'd only said they were 'squirty crying sobbers'.

LIES
IN THE WOODS

I'm sure you've heard the tale of poor little Hansel and Gretel. You've heard they were dumped in the woods by their cruel parents then captured by a witch. Well, that's a load of piffle and I hope you didn't believe it. That story is just a pack of lies that Hansel and Gretel cooked up to keep out of trouble.

Let's look at some of the outrageous fibs they told, and I'll tell you what I think really happened . . .

The first little lie

Hansel and Gretel's mother died and their father was married again, this time to a cruel woman who said the children were eating too much. The **wicked stepmother** told their father to take his children into the woods and get rid of them.

The truth

Hansel and Gretel's new stepmother was not at all wicked. They just said she was bad because they missed their mother.

What really happened

Hansel and Gretel's father was a woodcutter. His wife was too lazy to cook or clean. She ordered food every day from a takeaway called **Greasy Klaus**. The woodcutter, his wife and their children Hansel and Gretel ate Greasy Klaus food so often that they saved up a whole cupboard-full of special bonus vouchers so they could get more Greasy Klaus for free whenever they wanted it. The whole family became very fat.

Then one fine day Hansel and Gretel's
mother dropped dead. This was sad
because she wasn't very old and the
children did love her, but I'm afraid it's
what happens to people who eat too much
Greasy Klaus food.

Hansel and Gretel and their father were
very upset. Then, luckily, the woodcutter
fell in love with a beautiful lady called
Gloria. Gloria was fit and active, drank
lots of water and did exercises every day.

Soon Gloria and the woodcutter were married, and Gloria tried her very best to be a good stepmother to Hansel and Gretel. She bought them bicycles for their birthdays, but they were too lazy to use them. She encouraged them to exercise with her, but they didn't like getting hot and sweaty.

Instead of eating the nice food that Gloria made for them, Hansel and Gretel sneaked down to Greasy Klaus with their free special bonus food vouchers. They became fatter than ever.

One night Gloria said to the woodcutter, 'I'm very worried about the children eating too much and not getting enough exercise. We've got a beautiful forest right there on our back doorstep. Why not take them for a walk tomorrow?'

The next lie

The woodcutter left Hansel and Gretel in the forest **on purpose**.

The truth

It was Hansel and Gretel's own silly fault they got lost.

What really happened

It was a beautiful day for a walk. The woodcutter did most of his woodcutting inside in a big sawmill these days so he'd forgotten how lovely the forest was and how good it felt to be out in the fresh air. But Hansel and Gretel just whined and whinged.

'Are we there yet?' asked Gretel every three minutes.

'We're never going to get there,' said Hansel. 'There's nothing here but boring trees and green grass. I'm going back home.'

'But we don't know the way,' whined Gretel.

'We won't get lost,' said Hansel. 'You know those **disgusting** wholemeal bread sandwiches Gloria gave us for lunch? I crumbled mine up and threw them away bit by bit, so we can follow the line of bread back home.'

When their father disappeared round a bend in front of them, Hansel took Gretel by the hand and they ran back down the path, following the line of wholemeal breadcrumbs. But suddenly the line stopped. The birds of the forest, knowing that wholemeal crumbs taste **absolutely delicious**, had eaten them all.

'See, I told you so!' said Gretel, which is a really annoying thing little sisters always say. 'You've got us lost! We've got nothing to eat and nothing to drink, and I'm tired and my feet hurt . . . '

'Shut your gob, Gretel!' said Hansel, which is a really annoying and rude thing big brothers always say.

Yet another lie

Hansel and Gretel found a cottage made of gingerbread.

The truth

Nobody, and I mean *nobody*, would be stupid enough to build a cottage out of gingerbread. If you think about it for just a minute, you'd realise that as soon as it rained, a cottage made of gingerbread would get soft and soggy and fall to pieces, leaving just a gooey heap on the ground.

The cottage Hansel and Gretel found was made of wood, although it probably did have a sort of gingerbready colour. It was getting dark, remember, and Hansel and Gretel were very hungry, so they would have imagined anything looked like food.

What really happened

Hansel and Gretel wandered round in the forest for hours, until night began to fall.

'I'm so hungry I could eat a house,' said Hansel.

'You mean, you could eat a horse,' said Gretel.

'No, I could eat a house, like that one over there,' said Hansel. He stumbled across to the cottage and stuffed a piece of a windowsill into his mouth.

Just then, Hansel and Gretel heard a mysterious voice, saying, 'Nibble, nibble, nibble! Who's nibbling my little house!'

The door of the cottage opened and out came a tall thin woman with a long pointy nose.

110

One more absolutely huge lie

The woman with the pointy nose was a witch.

The truth

No, she wasn't. The lady who lived in the cottage was called Emily Green.

What really happened

The cottage Hansel and Gretel had found was part of a camp for kids, run by a nice lady called Emily Green. She called it the Happy Healthy Holiday Home, or '4H' for short. Every week, children flocked to the cottage in the forest to eat her delicious meals and play games in the fresh clean air. Emily Green ran lively and interesting cooking classes, to teach children that healthy food is not only good for you, but can be delicious and fun.

When kind Emily Green looked out the cottage window and saw a ℏungry little fat boy trying to eat her windowsill, she called him in at once. 'Who's trying to eat my little house?' called Emily Green. 'If you're really so hungry, come inside, you poor little darlings.'

'You look like an ugly old witch,' said Gretel rudely.

'And you look like a roly-poly pig,' Emily said back. She was used to dealing with cheeky children. Then she smiled sweetly. 'But you've come to the right place. A few days of healthy eating and you'll be fit enough to win gold medals in a fun run. You're just in time for dinner.' Of course, Hansel and Gretel didn't want to miss dinner, so they followed her inside.

113

Inside the house was a table on which stood a steaming **vegetable quiche**. 'No fat, no sugar, only good fresh ingredients and a little imagination,' said Emily Green, cutting them each a thick slice. 'Please eat as much as you want.'

Gretel was just about to take a nibble when Hansel said, 'Yuck! What are those weird orange bits?'

'Carrots,' said Emily Green, surprised that he didn't recognise them.

'And what's this yucky green stuff?' asked Gretel.

'Haven't you ever seen **broccoli** before?' asked Emily.

'No, and I never want to see it again!' said Gretel rudely. She pushed her plate off the table, where it *smashed*, scattering quiche across the kitchen floor.

Even more lies

The witch locked Hansel in a cage and made Gretel do all the housework.

The truth

She shut Hansel up for his own good. And, at a camp, **everybody** has to help with the chores.

What really happened

'Oops!' said Emily Green. 'That was bad luck dropping your plate like that, Gretel. But don't worry, you can clean it up after you've had your dinner.'

'Haven't you got any real food that we can eat?' said Hansel.

'What do you call "real food"?' asked Emily.

'Real, nice food,' said Hansel, 'like Greasy Klaus Megapizzas.'

'With **double fries**,' added Gretel.

'I'm sorry, darlings,' said Emily Green sweetly. 'Here at 4H we only have fresh food. But if you like pizzas, I'll teach you to cook them tomorrow. A good pizza made with healthy ingredients can be delicious as well as good for you.'

'You want us to cook food ourselves??!' screamed Hansel. 'Don't you know we're kids? And I'm a boy!!!'

'Cooking isn't hard, and it can be great fun,' said Emily Green. 'Lots of boys are very good at it. But tonight I won't force you to try food you haven't seen before. Leave the quiche and I'll get you some fresh fruit for dessert.' She disappeared into her pantry.

'That witch wants us to be her slaves,' whispered Hansel. 'Let's get out of here!'

'But what if we get lost in the forest again?' Gretel whispered back. 'We'll die.'

'If I don't find some proper food to eat, I'll die anyway,' said Hansel. He crept across to the door. It was locked.

'It's not safe to go out into the forest at night,' said Emily Green, returning with a basket of apples and oranges.

'Why not?' said Hansel.

'There are **wolves** and **bears** out there,' said Emily. 'Their habitat was destroyed by woodcutters, so we've made a wildlife sanctuary in this part of the forest.' She took Hansel's elbow and firmly pulled him back to the table. 'Eat your dinner.'

Hansel threw a total wobbly.
'**Let me go, you witch!**' he yelled. He struggled and kicked and tried to bite her.

'Ooh, temper, temper,' she trilled. 'I think someone needs to go to the Time Out Room.'

She shut Hansel up in a little bedroom with pillows stuck on all the walls so he couldn't hurt himself. 'Just stay here and think about what your problem is,' she said gently. 'We'll talk about it tomorrow when you feel calmer.'

Gretel was so hungry that she ate a slice of quiche and found it wasn't too bad after all. She even ate an apple for dessert.

Then Emily Green handed Gretel a
mop. 'Now, my girl, you made a mess with
your little tantrum. You clean it up.' Gretel
had never cleaned up anything in her life,
but Emily was very strict. 'At 4H
everybody has to help with the chores,'
she said. 'Those are the rules here.' She
made Gretel clean every last skerrick
of vegetable quiche off the floor then wash
the dishes before she went to bed.

The next lie

The witch wanted to cook Hansel in her oven and eat him.

The truth

Emily Green was a vegetarian. Hansel would have tasted horrible anyway, because of all the Greasy Klaus food he'd eaten in his lifetime.

How it happened

Next morning when Gretel woke up, the table was set for breakfast. There were juicy peaches and apricots, bowls of muesli and a jug of fresh orange juice so cool that beads of moisture were condensing on the outside. Hansel was already sitting at the table looking very grumpy.

'Good morning, Gretel,' said Emily Green brightly. 'I hope you slept well.'

'No, I didn't,' said Gretel. 'My pillow was much too hard.' In fact she'd slept very well, but she didn't want to admit it.

'I was awake all night too,' grumbled Hansel. 'That mattress in the Time Out Room must be made of rocks.'

'Never mind,' said Emily, 'I have a surprise for you. I think you'll find it's fun and refreshing. Just the thing to wake you up in the morning.'

She opened a little door in the wall and the children saw a fire burning brightly in there. Emily tossed a lump of wood into the fire and slammed the door shut.

Above the little fire door was a much larger door, with steps leading up to it. Emily Green climbed up the steps and opened the larger door. 'Nearly hot enough,' she said. 'Hansel, why don't you go first?'

Hansel and Gretel shrank back against the wall. They'd seen a door over a fire just like this before. It was the pizza oven at Greasy Klaus. Now they were sure that Emily was a witch, and they knew why she'd wanted them to eat her food. She was fattening them up to cook them in her oven!

'This is the perfect place for you two,' said Emily Green. 'Open the door for me, Gretel, and we'll see if it's hot enough for Hansel.'

Gretel still hung back. 'I don't understand,' she said. 'What exactly do you want me to do?'

'It really is very simple, you $silly$ $girl$!' said Emily, opening the door herself. 'All you do is open the door and stick your head in to see if it's hot enough, and then . . . hey, what are you doing?!'

Gretel had pushed her in the back. Emily Green stumbled in through the door above the fire, and Gretel quickly **slammed** it shut.

The lie
The witch burned up in the oven.

The truth
Wrong again.

How it happened

Emily Green was locked in. She heard the cottage door slam, then Hansel and Gretel's footsteps crunching over the grass as they ran out into the forest.

If you were locked in a pizza oven, and let's hope you never are, you would die. But Emily Green didn't die, because the pizza oven wasn't a pizza oven at all; it was a $sauna$ room, warmed by the log fire. Hansel and Gretel had never seen a sauna room before, so they couldn't be expected to know what one looked like. All the same, it wasn't easy for Emily Green to get out. She had to wait in the sauna room, sweating and sweating, until eventually she lost so much weight that she was able to squeeze out through the sauna window and hop into a refreshing $icy \ bath$ to cool herself down.

She wondered whether she ought to run after Hansel and Gretel, to bring them back to the cottage in case they met a wild animal. Then she remembered what **unpleasant little brats** they'd been, so she shrugged and said to herself, 'I hope they meet a wolf.'

The lie

Hansel and Gretel lived happily ever after.

The truth

Oh no, they didn't.

The lie

Oh yes, they did!

The truth

That would be just too easy for them. They'd done lots of **selfish** and **stupid** things and, to make matters worse, when they got home they spread nasty rumours about nice Emily Green being a witch who ate little kids.

WHAT HAPPENED
EVER AFTER . . .

Sadly, mud sticks. Many people believed
Hansel and Gretel's lies, so poor Emily
had to close down the Happy Healthy
Holiday Home and move to another state
because most children were afraid of
getting eaten by the witch.
As to what happened to Hansel and
Gretel after that, I really don't know.
Maybe their stepmother Gloria managed
to teach them to be good, and if so,
maybe they did live happily ever after.
But personally, I doubt it.

BENJAMIN BOGGLE'S BEANS

Sometimes people pass through a fairytale so fast we don't even learn their names. We call them 'minor characters' and don't pay them much attention. But if we knew a bit more about them, we'd realise how important these people are. Without them, the story might be very different . . .

Once upon a time, a boy called Benjamin
Boggle lived with his mother in a poor
cottage. They didn't have much money but
they had enough to eat because Benjamin
grew beans – red beans and green
beans, yellow beans and purple
beans, and rare Bolivian Bouncing
beans, which were fun to play with at the
dinner table.

Every Saturday, Benjamin loaded a
sack of beans into his wheelbarrow and
went off to market to sell them. Benjamin
and Mrs Boggle were poor but happy –
until the Very Bad Bean Year.

In the **Very Bad Bean Year,** Benjamin Boggle's beans wouldn't grow, no matter what he did. Benjamin weeded the bean patch and watered the beanstalks every day. But the leaves on the spindly little vines were yellow and drooping, and they hardly grew any beans at all.

Then came the day when Benjamin Boggle picked the last few **shrivelled** bean pods from his last shrivelled beanstalk. Mrs Boggle cooked a thin bean soup and sighed, 'This is no good, Benjamin, you'll have to look for another job.'

'But I love growing beans, Mum,' said Benjamin.

'I know you do,' said Mrs Boggle, 'but beans that won't grow are no good to anyone. We've got just **five beans** left over. Take them to market and see what you can get for them.'

🫘 🫘 🫘 🫘 🫘

Next morning Benjamin Boggle set off for the market with his five miserable beans in a little bag.

It was a hot sunny day and, not far down the road, Benjamin met a boy, beating a skinny cow to keep her moving.

'Hey,' said Benjamin. 'Leave that poor cow alone! Can't you see she's tired?'

'I'm tired too,' said the boy. 'It's far too hot for walking into town.'

'Then why are you going there?' asked Benjamin Boggle.

'Because I have to take this cow and sell her at the market, stupid!' said the boy rudely. 'Why don't you buy her if you love her so much? You won't regret it. She's, um, a magic cow.'

'Really?' said Benjamin, 'What's
𝔪𝔞𝔤𝔦𝔠 about her?'

The boy's eyes flicked from side to side.
'Buy her and you'll find out,' he said.

'I don't have any money,' said Benjamin.

'What've you got in that bag?' snapped
the boy.

Benjamin Boggle showed the boy his
beans. You can probably guess what
happened next.

When Benjamin Boggle came home, his mother wasn't pleased. 'You silly boy! Why did you buy a miserable skinny cow that will never give any milk? And what are we going to feed her?'

'I felt sorry for her,' shrugged Benjamin, 'Her name is Poppy. The boy who sold her to me said she was a magic cow.'

Mrs Boggle sighed. 'Benjamin Boggle, that boy was lying. There's no such thing as a magic cow!'

'I know,' said Benjamin. 'And I had to tell him my beans were magic too, so he'd do me a swap.'

Just then there was a horrible, squelchy sound behind him and Poppy did a ploppy. A big, brown, stinking, steaming, sloppy ploppy, right on the doormat.

'That does it, Benjamin!' said his mum firmly. 'Take that cow out to the garden! Tomorrow you're going back to sell her at the market. And clean up that ploppy!'

Benjamin Boggle scraped the ploppy off the mat with a shovel, and tossed it on the bean patch. Then he tied the cow up next to the straggly beanstalk.

'I'm sorry, Poppy,' he said. 'Mum's right. We don't have any food for you to eat. We don't even have any beans for our own supper.'

Next morning, Mrs Boggle screeched at Benjamin through his bedroom window, 'Benjamin Boggle, come and look at this!!!'

Benjamin jumped out of bed and ran outside.

Poppy the cow was happily chomping on giant beans! They hung from a beanstalk with glossy green leaves and pods as thick as Benjamin's arm. The beanstalk towered above the house and its head disappeared into the clouds. Its roots disappeared too, into the middle of Poppy's ploppy.

Benjamin Boggle gasped, 'Poppy, you really are a magic cow! Your ploppies make the best bean fertiliser in the whole world!'

'Amazing!' said Mrs Boggle. 'Pick some beans, Benjamin, and we'll have a big baked bean breakfast.'

But before Benjamin could pick a single bean, the beanstalk began to tremble. A voice above them boomed, 'Fee fi fo fum! I feel a rumbling in my tum!' An enormous boot came crashing down through the leaves.

Benjamin and Mrs Boggle rushed inside the cottage, slammed the door shut and hid under the bed.

Heavy footsteps clumped towards them. **Thump! Thump! Thump!** The voice roared, 'Anybody 'ome?'

'No!' called Benjamin.

'Shh, you silly boy!' whispered Mrs Boggle.

A giant eye appeared at the window. Benjamin and his mother could see the giant eye. The giant eye could see them too. 'I want some beans,' said the giant voice.

'Just what we needed!' whispered Mrs Boggle to Benjamin. 'A giant bean thief!'

'Take as many beans as you like!' called Benjamin. 'Then go away, please.'

'I can pay for 'em,' said the giant. The giant eye disappeared from the window. In its place appeared a giant hand, holding up a golden egg.

Benjamin crawled out from under the bed and opened the door. The giant thrust the golden egg into his hand. 'I hope it's enough,' said the giant. 'My hen only lays one egg a day, and I already spent yesterday's egg buying socks.'

'It's more than enough, thank you,' said Benjamin.

'Phew, that's a relief,' sighed the giant.
'Your beans look delicious. It's hard to get
'em in my size. Socks and beans, I mean.
The name's Norm, by the way.'

He held out his giant hand, and
Benjamin shook his giant little finger. 'You
come and buy beans any time, Norm,' he
said. 'We'll have plenty more by
tomorrow.'

Benjamin held a sack open, and Norm
filled it with giant beans from the
beanstalk, grinning, 'Fee fi fo fum, I
love beans, so back I'll come.'

Then Norm slung the sack on his back and tiptoed across the bean patch.

'Fee fi fo fum, don't step in ploppies from an old cow's bum!' he laughed.

Benjamin laughed too. 'Sorry about those ploppies, Norm, but they sure make the beans grow.'

Norm climbed up the beanstalk again, calling back, 'See you tomorrow!'

But Norm didn't come back the next
morning, or the next day either.

'Maybe he didn't like the beans,' said
Mrs Boggle. 'Maybe he's in bed with food
poisoning . . . '

Then just as it was getting dark, Norm
arrived. He didn't come climbing down
the beanstalk this time; he was
limping along the road. His trouser leg
was torn and his knee was bloody. He'd
been crying.

Benjamin sat him down on the
woodheap, and Mrs Boggle wiped the
blood off his knee with a wet towel.

'What happened to you, Norm?' asked Benjamin.

'I been robbed,' said Norm. '. . . and I nearly been murdered too.'

'Murdered?' said the Boggles together.

Norm told them his sad tale, most of which you've probably heard before. 'Yesterday, this kid snuck into my castle in the clouds, and he stole my hen what lays them special eggs, then this morning I finds him nicking my special harp what plays by itself. I tries to catch him, but he runs to a giant beanstalk and climbs down.'

'He climbed down our beanstalk?'
asked Benjamin.

'Nah,' said Norm. 'He's got this other
beanstalk, going down to his back garden.
I starts climbing down after him but what
does he do? Chops the beanstalk from
under me, that's what!'

'How awful!' said Mrs
Boggle, tipping a whole
bottle of
disinfectant onto
Norm's cut knee.

'Ooh!' gasped
Norm, 'That stuff
stings! Anyways, I
had a really horrible
fall. I had to pretend
to be dead all day.'

'Why?' asked Benjamin.

Norm shuffled uncomfortably. 'In case he tried to finish me off,' he muttered. 'You know these criminal types. He had an axe. Anyways, now I can't bring you no more golden eggs, and I can't buy no more beans.'

Benjamin Boggle took a deep breath. 'Norm,' said Benjamin, 'you take as many beans as you want, and pay me when you can. But first, show me where this guy lives.'

When they came to the cottage, Norm hovered nervously in the background, trying not to be noticed. That's not an easy thing for a giant to do. Benjamin skirted around the huge tangle of fallen beanstalk lying across the garden. When he stepped in an old cow ploppy, he guessed why this beanstalk had also grown so big.

Benjamin knocked on the door. It was opened by the boy who'd sold Poppy to Benjamin. 'Yes?' he snapped.

'You stole Norm's hen and his harp,' said Benjamin.

'Taking things from giants isn't stealing,' said the boy, **rudely pointing** his finger at Norm. 'He probably stole them from someone else.'

'I didn't steal them,' said Norm. 'I bought 'em from a **wizard school fete**. I got receipts and everything.'

An old woman appeared behind the boy. 'Give them back, Jack,' she said. 'They've caused us nothing but trouble. The hen's never laid us an egg, and that dratted harp's been driving me mad. For the last three hours it's been playing Incy Wincy Spider.'

'My favourite song,' said Norm shyly.

Jack disappeared into the house and came out clutching an indignant brown hen and a battered golden harp.

'Master! Master!' called the harp when it saw Norm.

'It's all right, darlings,' said Norm,
'Daddy's here.' He slipped the harp into
one pocket and the hen into another.

'So what do we do now, Mum?' wailed
Jack. 'We've got no money, no cow and I
don't have a job.'

Benjamin Boggle smiled.
'I know a job that you could do, Jack,'
he said.

WHAT HAPPENED EVER AFTER . . .

It's all worked out quite well.
Every day, Norm buys Benjamin
Boggle's beans using golden eggs, and
Mrs Boggle sells the eggs in the town.
Benjamin loves planting and watering
his beans and inventing new varieties.
It's hard work, but now he has an
assistant. Jack comes to the bean patch
every day. His job is to spread Poppy's
magic ploppies.

Richard Tulloch has
written over sixty children's books,
heaps of plays and numerous scripts
for children's TV series, including the
famous *Bananas in Pyjamas* and *New
McDonald's Farm*. He has two grown-
up children, lives with his wife in Sydney and spends
part of each year based in Amsterdam. In between
times, he travels the world, performing his storytelling
show *Storyman* and teaching writing workshops in
schools.

Terry Denton is one of those
lucky people who can both write and
illustrate. He has written sixteen
children's books and collaborated on
thirty more with some of the most
popular children's authors in Australia.
Some of his best known books are the
Andy Griffiths *Just!* series, his own
Gasp! series and his new *Wombat and Fox: Tales of
the city*. Terry lives by the beach with his wife and
three kids.

Don't miss BEASTLY TALES,
six crazy creature capers
from this dynamic team.